For Dave and Brian
with thanks to Dan
—J.M.

For Linda
— W.W.

Text copyright © 2004 by Jean Marzollo.
Photographs © 1992 by Walter Wick.

All rights reserved. Published by Scholastic Inc.
SCHOLASTIC, CARTWHEEL BOOKS, and associated logos
are trademarks and/or registered trademarks of Scholastic Inc.
Lexile is a registered trademark of MetaMetrics, Inc.

All images by Walter Wick taken from I Spy Christmas.
Published by Scholastic Inc. in 1992.

Library of Congress Cataloging-in-Publication Data
Marzollo, Jean.
I spy a candy cane / riddles by Jean Marzollo ; photographs by Walter Wick.
    p. cm. — (Scholastic reader. Level 1)
"Cartwheel Books."
ISBN 0-439-52474-1
1. Picture puzzles — Juvenile literature. I. Wick, Walter, ill. II. Title. III. Series.
GV1507.P47M28 2004
793.73 — dc22
2004004732   CIP

ISBN-13: 978-0-439-52474-2
ISBN-10: 0-439-52474-1
30 29 28 27 26   40   11 12
Printed in the U.S.A. 23 • This edition first printing, August 2008

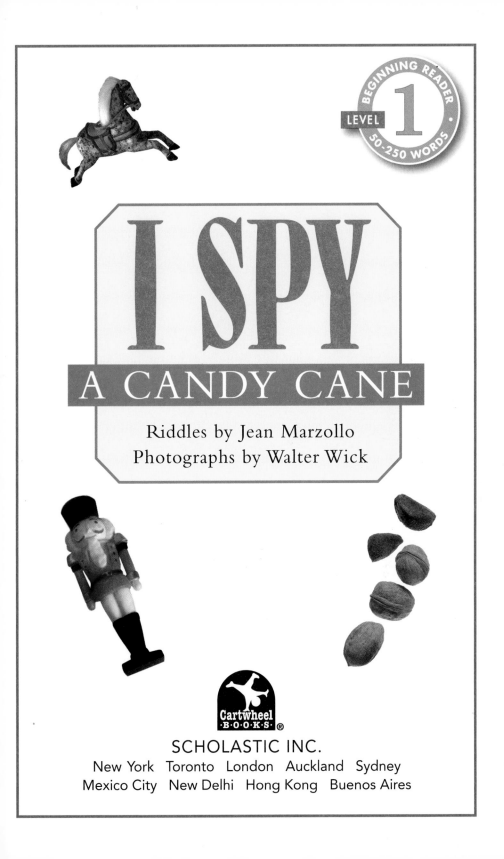

I SPY

A CANDY CANE

Riddles by Jean Marzollo
Photographs by Walter Wick

Cartwheel
·B·O·O·K·S·®

SCHOLASTIC INC.
New York Toronto London Auckland Sydney
Mexico City New Delhi Hong Kong Buenos Aires

I spy

 a red roof,

eight reindeer,

 a Y,

a French horn,

 an apple,

and a bright blue fly.

I spy  a horse,

three gumdrops,

a J,

a rope,

and a sock that's
red and gray.

I spy

two candles meant
for a cake,

two golden bells,

 and a pretty snowflake.

I spy

a flag,

 a tiny yellow bear,

an ice-cream cone,

 and a face with
white hair.

I spy

a mallet,

a cookie-cutter tree,

 strawberry leaves,

and some cherries for me.

I spy

a giraffe,

a gift box,

 a king,

a green paint jar,

and popcorn string.

I spy

 a 4,

a blanket,

 a steeple,

a tiara,

 and a bus for
tiny people.

a candle,

 a snake,

a 2,

 a shiny moon,

and a sleigh that's blue.

I spy

a snowman,

 a horn,

a key,

 a spider's web,

and an icicle tree.

I spy

 a drum,

a zebra's mane,

 a man with
a tree,

and a candy cane.

I spy 2 matching words.

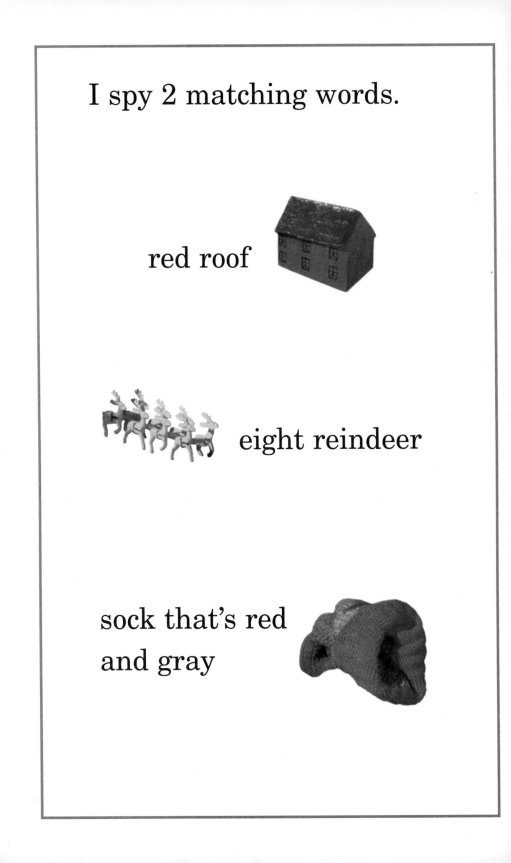

red roof

eight reindeer

sock that's red and gray

I spy 2 matching words.

 man with
a tree

two golden bells

 face with white hair

I spy 2 words that start with the letter G.

giraffe

three gumdrops

 and a bright blue fly

I spy 2 words that start with the letters ST.

strawberry leaves

a king

steeple

I spy 2 words that end
with the letter Y.

a candle

 bus for tiny people

candy cane

I spy 2 words that end
with the letter R.

 eight reindeer

bear

 a horn

I spy 2 words that rhyme.

two candles
meant for a cake

snake

 mallet

I spy 2 words that rhyme.

key

a flag

icicle tree